Based on the TV series Nickelodeon Avatar: The Last Airbender™ as seen on Nickelodeon®

SIMON SPOTLIGHT

An imprint of Simon & Schuster Children's Publishing Division

1230 Avenue of the Americas, New York, New York 10020

© 2007 Viacom International Inc. All rights reserved. NICKELODEON, Nickelodeon Avatar: The Last Airbender, and all related titles, logos, and characters are trademarks of Viacom International Inc.

All rights reserved, including the right of reproduction in whole or in part in any form. SIMON SPOTLIGHT and colophon are registered trademarks of Simon & Schuster, Inc.

Nontoxic

Manufactured in the United States of America

First Edition

1 2 3 4 5 6 7 8 9 10

ISBN-13: 978-1-4169-3606-0

ISBN-10: 1-4169-3606-8

Library of Congress Catalog Card Number 2006937729

THE EARTH KINGDOM CHRONICLES:
THE TALE OF
AANG

by Michael Teitelbaum
based on original screenplays
written for *Avatar: The Last Airbender*
illustrated by Patrick Spaziante

Simon Spotlight/Nickelodeon
New York London Toronto Sydney

Chapter 1

My name is Aang. I'm the Avatar. I'm also 5 an Airbender. My friend Katara has been teaching me Waterbending. She's become an amazing Waterbender!

Katara and her brother, Sokka, are traveling with me, helping me to master all four elements—air, water, earth, and fire—so I can defeat Fire Lord Ozai and the Fire Nation, and bring peace to the four nations. All in a day's work for the Avatar, right?

Next on my list is to learn Earthbending. So Katara, Sokka, my lemur Momo, and I are flying on my sky bison, Appa, to the city of Omashu in the Earth Kingdom to find my old pal King Bumi. I can't wait to learn Earthbending from him!

☯ ☯ ☯

Our first stop was General Fong's Earth Kingdom base. He was supposed to give us an escort to make sure we made it to Omashu safely, but it didn't quite work out that way. General Fong had this crazy idea that he could force me into the Avatar state, and then I could go and fight the Fire Nation. He said that while I learn the elements, the war goes on. I started to think that maybe he was right, that maybe I could end the war now if I let him help me. Boy, was I wrong! Katara helped me realize how dangerous being in the Avatar state really is, especially when I can't control it. Even she's scared of me when I'm in it—that says a lot.

So I told General Fong that I wouldn't force the Avatar state. He flipped out! He told his Earth Kingdom soldiers to attack me so he could force me into it against my will. And when that didn't work, he attacked Katara. He started Earth-bending her into the ground, so she was sink-ing. I was so angry and upset about Katara that the general got his wish: I went into the Avatar state, even though it took me a while to get into it. When I was in it, Avatar Roku, the previous Avatar, came to me. He told me that the Avatar state is a defense mechanism that gives me the skills and knowledge of all the past Avatars. In the Avatar state, all the spirits of past Avatars are within me. That is why I'm so powerful. But they are all exposed to whatever danger I face. If I'm killed while in the Avatar state, then all of the past Avatars will die with me. The reincarnation cycle will be broken and the Avatar will cease to exist. Pretty heavy, huh?

When I came out of the Avatar state, Katara was fine. I learned that Fong was just using her to trick me into going into the Avatar state. We finally managed to get away from him, thanks to Sokka, who snuck up behind him and conked him on the head with a club.

Anyway, after that was settled, we climbed onto the back of Appa, my flying bison. We're flying off toward Omashu—without an escort.

I'm trying not to think about what Roku told me—you know, about what would happen if I died in the Avatar state. Instead I'm turning my thoughts to Omashu and my old pal Bumi!

Chapter 2

8 After traveling for miles, Appa landed so we could rest for a bit. Katara was showing me a new Waterbending move called the Octopus. Things were going great until she put her arms around me to correct my form and I forgot everything I was doing and lost myself in her eyes. I can't help it—they're just so pretty! Anyway, that's when this singing and dancing group came walking out of the nearby woods. They told us they were nomads. We decided to travel with them to Omashu through these secret tunnels and caves that one of them, Chong, told us about. The tunnels cut through

the mountain and lead directly to Omashu.

As we entered the caves, Chong told us about the legend of the two lovers. He also told us that the caves were cursed.

"Only those who trust in love can make it through the caves. Everyone else gets trapped forever."

Hmm. All we have to do is trust in love? Something tells me that's harder than it sounds. . . .

As soon as we stepped into the cave, a rockslide sealed off the entrance. We wandered through the tunnels for hours. Then a wolfbat attacked. I sent an Airbending blast at it, which knocked Sokka's flaming torch from his hand and onto Appa, who started kicking wildly. I'd never seen him so upset! Katara put out the fire just as Appa kicked the cave walls and rocks came tumbling down from the ceiling. I managed to get Sokka and the nomads out of the way in time, but then the rest of the ceiling came crashing down, and I had to grab Katara and fly us to the other side of the cave. After the crash, I found myself on the ground next to Katara with my arm around her.

What are the odds? I wish I could stay like

this forever . . . but I have to get up and make sure everyone's okay. Looks like Appa's okay, and Katara is too, but what's that huge wall of rocks? Oh, no! The wall has separated us from Sokka and the nomads. I guess they're going to have to find their own way out of the tunnel—I have to focus on finding a safe way out for Appa, Katara, and me.

⊕ ⊕ ⊕

We'd been walking through the dark tunnels for hours when we came across a large stone door. We pushed through the door, but instead of an exit, there was a tomb—two tombs actually.

Katara noticed that the pictures on the tomb walls told the lovers' story. They were from warring villages on opposite sides of the mountain. Because of the war, the lovers had to meet in secret. They learned Earthbending from the badger moles so they could Earthbend these tunnels and caves to get to one another. Then the man was killed in the war. Instead of destroying both villages with her Earthbending power, the woman forced the two villages to stop the war and together they built a new city. The woman's name was Oma. The man's name was

Shu. And so the new city was named Omashu to honor their love.

"It says here 'Love is brightest in the dark,'" Katara read.

Her torch is starting to fade. Soon we'll be trapped in total darkness. For the first time since we entered the caves, I'm worried. Still, I don't want Katara to know how nervous I am. Just stay calm, and everything will be fine.

"I have a crazy idea," Katara said suddenly.

"What?" I hope it's a good one, because this place is giving me the creeps!

"Never mind," she said, turning away.

It's pretty dark in here, but is Katara blush-ing? It sure looks like it.

"It's too crazy."

"Katara, what is it?" One of us better come up with something soon. . . .

"Well, the curse says that we'll be trapped in here forever unless we trust in love. And above this picture of them kissing it says 'Love is brightest in the dark.' So, what if we kissed?"

Uh . . . did I just hear her right? Katara and me, kiss? Katara wants to kiss me? Almost since the moment I met her I've dreamed of kissing her. Did she really say that?

"Us, kissing?" I need to be sure I actually heard her right.

"See, that was a crazy idea," she said quickly.

This is going to be the best day of my life! I can't move, breathe, or smile, but I've never been more excited in my life! I think I may pass out. . . .

"Us. Kissing." Okay, stop saying that and just say yes before she changes her—

"Us, kissing!" Katara repeated, laughing loudly. "What was I thinking? Can you imagine that!"

It's too late. I blew it! Standing here in my daze I let the moment pass and now she's tak—ing the crazy wonderful suggestion back . . . like she wishes she never said it. Now I have to act that way too. I mean, I can't let her know that I think it's the greatest idea she ever had. Just smile, and try to sound like you agree with her.

"I definitely wouldn't want to kiss you!" Oh, no. I wish I could take that back. What a dumb thing to say! And I don't even mean it!

"Oh, well I didn't realize it was such a hor—rible option," Katara said harshly. "Sorry I suggested it."

Great, now she's mad. Why do I say such dumb things! I have to make this right.

"No, no, I mean if it's a choice between kissing you and dying, I—" Oh boy, that didn't help. I just can't get it right when it comes to Katara. Okay, let's try again.

"I'm saying I would rather kiss you than die. That's a compliment."

"Well, I'm not sure which I would rather do!"

And now she's storming out of the tomb. Great. Instead of fixing things, I just keep making them worse. Why am I so afraid to let Katara know how I feel about her? Now it doesn't matter. I really blew it.

"We're going to run out of light any second now, aren't we?" I asked, catching up to her.

"I think so."

At least she's still talking to me. "Then what are we going to do?"

"What can we do?" She turned toward me. Just then her light went out.

Here we are in pitch dark with no hope

of ever getting out, except to believe in the legend. To believe in love. I'm just going to go for it. Come on Aang, just be brave. What do you have to lose? Just lean in and . . .

Whoa! What's that path of light on the ceiling? I guess love really will show us the way! The lights look like some kind of crystal.

"They must only light up in the dark!" I realized.

"That's what they meant by love being brightest in the dark!" Katara exclaimed. "That's how the two lovers found each other. They put out their lights and followed the crystals."

So we followed the crystals all the way out of the caves. A moment after we exited, we saw Sokka and the nomads riding badger moles out of the cave. Then we said good-bye to the nomads and went on our way.

We are so close to Omashu, I can smell it! Just over this big hill and there it—no! I can't believe my eyes. There, draped over the main wall of the great Earth Kingdom city of Omashu, is a gigantic Fire Nation flag!

Things haven't exactly been going according to plan since we started this journey through the Earth Kingdom, and getting Bumi to teach me Earthbending was another one of those things. Even though Omashu was taken over by the Fire Nation, I insisted on going in any—way to find Bumi.

On our way through the city, we got attacked by a Firebender and ended up bumping into the Earth Kingdom resistance. I asked them about Bumi, and they said he surrendered the city on the first day of the invasion. That didn't sound like my old pal Bumi, so I didn't believe them at first, but now it makes more sense. See, while I looked for Bumi, Sokka and Katara evacuated the Earth Kingdom residents from the city by pre—tending they had all been infected with pentapox. Pentapi are harmless creatures that stick to you and make big purple marks on your skin—but the Fire Nation didn't know that! They thought the purple marks were contagious and let all the citizens leave. As they were leaving, Katara and Sokka noticed that the baby boy of the newly appointed Fire Nation governor of Omashu had followed them out of the city. We decided to have a trade—off: the baby for King Bumi. But just as we were about to make the trade, another

Firebender stepped forward and called it off. Then they pulled Bumi away. I chased after him, and in between dodging flying fireballs, I was able to have a brief talk with my old friend.

He told me that in addition to the positive and negative jings, or techniques, of attacking and retreating used in the bending arts, Earthbending also requires a neutral jing, which involves listening and waiting for the right moment to strike. He's using the neutral jing, just waiting for the right moment to attack. Then he'll take back Omashu when the Fire Nation least expects it. That sounds more like Bumi! He won't be teaching me Earthbending, but he did tell me I need to find someone who has mastered neutral jing. I need to find a teacher who waits and listens before striking.

I wonder when I'm going to see my old friend Bumi again . . . but in the meantime, I'm on a mission to find an Earthbending teacher who waits and listens before striking, just like Bumi said.

Chapter 3

We flew over the Earth Kingdom, not really sure where we were headed next. As we passed over a swamp, I heard it calling to me, telling me to land. I figured if I was actually hearing the Earth, I probably shouldn't ignore it.

A few seconds later, a fierce wind pulled us down toward the swamp. By the time we landed, we had all gotten separated. While I was on my own, I had this vision of a laughing girl in a white dress. She seemed to want me to follow her, and she just kept laughing as I chased her through the swamp. Then she disappeared.

The wind turned out to just be a Waterbender who was trying to protect the swamp. He told us that the swamp is actually just one giant tree that is connected to everything, that the entire world is connected, and that time is an illusion.

But if time really is an illusion, maybe the girl I saw was someone I will meet in the future. Sokka and Katara also had visions, only theirs were of people from their past. Hmm . . . sometimes I wish I were just plain smarter. It would sure come in handy as the Avatar!

Anyway, we left the swamp and went to the town of Gaoling to Master Yu's Earthbending Academy in search of a teacher. But all Master Yu did was try to sell me more lessons. That's when I realized he's definitely not the one!

Then I heard about an Earthbending tournament called Earth Rumble Six, where the top Earthbenders in town competed against one another. So we went to watch. It was like nothing I'd ever seen! Xin Fu, who was running it, kept introducing Earthbenders with names like the Boulder and the Gopher. Boy, were they huge! The Boulder had beaten everyone in sight so far! At first I thought the Boulder was the champion, but I really couldn't see him being the teacher Bumi was talking about. I'm pretty sure the Boulder doesn't ever wait or listen. Oh, here comes the Boulder's final opponent—she's a twelve-year-old blind girl! She calls herself the Blind Bandit. SHE'S actually the reigning champion. She must be incredible. I can't wait to watch her!

Just then the Blind Bandit began to laugh defiantly.

Wait a second—I've heard that laugh before! She's the girl from my vision in the swamp! The vision really was of someone from the future. I guess I'm pretty smart after all!

Then the most incredible thing yet happened—the Blind Bandit beat the Boulder! Every time the Boulder took a step, the Blind Bandit knew exactly where he was. She shifted her weight from one foot to the other. The small movement was powerful enough to create a ripple in the ground, which rushed toward the Boulder like a wave. As he put his foot down, the wave struck it, causing him to hit the ground with his legs split wide apart. Then the Blind Bandit forced three stone spikes to burst from the ground, slamming into the Boulder and knocking him from the ring. The match was over in a matter of seconds.

"Winner and still champion, the Blind Bandit!" Xin Fu shouted from the center of the arena.

"How did she do that?" Katara asked.

The answer struck me at once. "She waited, and she listened." Just like Bumi said.

Then the announcer offered gold to anyone from the audience who could beat her, and I volunteered. I just wanted to get close enough to ask her to be my Earthbending teacher, but she kept knocking me with Earthbending moves. Finally I had to knock her down with an Airbending blow. She was pretty angry and stormed out of the arena.

🈷 🈷 🈷

We finally tracked her down as a member of the Beifong family. She's royalty! Pretty strange, huh? Anyway, we traveled to the house of Lao and Poppy Beifong. What a mansion! It's on a huge estate with gardens, servants, and everything. I announced myself as the Avatar, and Katara, Sokka, and I were invited in for dinner. At the dinner table sat the Blind Bandit, whose real name is Toph Beifong. Master Yu, the head of the Earthbending Academy, was there too. He's Toph's Earthbending teacher—like she needs one!

Anyway, it turned out that her parents didn't have a clue how powerful an Earthbender she is. They still thought she was a beginner! After dinner she told me that even though her parents saw her blindness as a handicap and were more protective of her because of it, she's always been able to see by using her Earthbending. She feels vibrations through her feet and that tells her everything she needs to know—and way more than most of us can see.

In the end, she had to tell her parents the truth because we were ambushed by the Earthbenders from Earth Rumble Six—they wanted to steal back the gold I had won. It all worked out though, and Toph agreed to be my teacher! I'm so excited. I think she's going to be exactly the teacher that Bumi wanted me to have.

We're off on Appa, again, and for the first time in a while, things are finally starting to look up.

Chapter 4

22 One night in our camp, Toph rushed from her tent and woke us all. "There's something coming toward us."

Her supersensitive feet were picking up vibrations of something rumbling closer and closer.

"Should we leave?" Katara asked.

"Nature seems to think so," I said, watching tons of animals flee from the woods in terror. "Let's go."

We all climbed onto Appa and took off into the night sky. I caught a glimpse of what was chasing us. It was this strange machine made of metal and shaped like a tank, coughing up black smoke. I didn't know what it was, but I had a really bad feeling about it.

No matter how far or fast we went, it kept finding us! I finally guided Appa up a high mountain to a steep cliff.

It followed us to three different places before we finally decided to stand our ground and see who or what it was. Turns out it was these three Fire Nation girls who we had dealt with in Omashu, including the Firebender who had chased Bumi and me through the Omashu mail chutes. They began galloping toward us. Toph unleashed some spectacular Earthbending moves to block them, but they dodged the huge rocks and kept on coming. It was clear to me that we weren't going to stop them. So once again we climbed aboard Appa and took off.

I know how tired I am. I can only imagine how exhausted Appa must be, carrying all of us, flying all night with no sleep. Hmm . . . I wonder why it feels like we're flying downward? Appa! He's dozing off! Okay, now we have to land, no matter what. Appa needs to rest!

On the ground, Katara and Toph started arguing about whose fault all of this was.

"If this is anyone's fault, it's 'sheddy' over there," Toph yelled, pointing at Appa. "He's been shedding his fur and leaving a trail for those girls to follow!"

I can't believe my ears! That's so unfair! I don't care if she is my Earthbending teacher. Nobody talks about Appa like that when I'm around. "How dare you blame Appa! He saved your life three times today! You always talk about how you carry your own weight, but you don't. Appa does. He carries your weight. And you know what? He never had a problem flying when it was just the three of us!"

Oops. I think I went a bit too far. I didn't really mean it. I'm just exhausted, and I don't like anyone saying bad things about Appa. Still, I was a bit harsh. . . . I wonder what she'll say. . . .

"See ya," she said finally. Then she picked up her bag and disappeared into the forest.

"I can't believe I yelled at my Earthbending teacher and now she's gone. I just tossed away my best chance of beating the Fire lord, of saving the world . . . of doing my job as the Avatar."

"I was pretty mean to her too," Katara admitted. "We need to find her and apologize."

The worst part is, it turns out Toph is right! Appa is shedding like crazy. Now that I look I can see his fur everywhere. I need to come up with a plan. . . .

First we washed Appa's shedding fur off in the river so that he wouldn't leave another trail. Then I told Katara and Sokka to take Appa and go find Toph. Meanwhile I grabbed a bunch of Appa's fur and flew around, leaving a fake trail in a totally different direction. This way if the tank follows the fur, it will be way off course. I hope I can make things right with Toph, but first I've got to stop those girls.

After flying around spreading Appa's fur, I landed in this town in the middle of nowhere. It's completely deserted. I should probably leave, but the thing is, I can't keep running forever, can I? I can't lose sight of my bigger mission. The time has come to face whoever is after me.

I think I'll just sit here and wait for them to find me, and find out what they're after. What's that sound? It's the Firebender! "All right, you've caught up with me. Now, who are you and what do you want?" It's time to settle this once and for all.

"Don't you see the family resemblance?" she asked. Then she covered one eye with her hand and said in a low gravelly voice, "I must find the Avatar to restore my honor."

Zuko! She sounds just like him. And now that I look closely, she looks kind of like him too. Is she Zuko's sister? Did they send her to track me down now? Did something bad happen to Zuko, and she took his place? Come to think of it, I haven't run into Zuko in a while. . . . Wait a minute, why am I worried about Zuko? He's devoted his life to trying to capture me for the Fire Nation. Besides, I'm the one in danger! I wonder if she's as powerful as he is.

"So, what now?" Let's see what she's made of.

"Now it's over," she said. "You can run, but I'll always catch you."

Like brother, like sister. "I'm not running."

"Do you really want to fight me?"

"Yes, I really do."

Okay, I know I didn't say that. Who—Zuko? Where did he come from? Has he been following me too? Are they going to team up against me?

"Back off, Azula," Zuko threatened. "He's mine."

Just back away slowly. The last thing I need is to face two Firebenders at the same time. Still, it doesn't seem like they're going to fight me as a team. They don't seem to like each other very much. It must be tough for Zuko to have a sister who seems so coldhearted. Wait a second—do I actually feel sorry for Zuko? Is that possible?

"I can see you two have a lot of catching up to do," I said. "So I'll just be going."

I guess I shouldn't have said anything. Just then, both Zuko and Azula turned toward me.

I can't escape. I'll have to battle them both. Zuko looks more anxious than me. Is he afraid of his sister? Azula is just smiling—her smile makes my skin crawl. There's no way out of this without fighting—I just hope I have the strength to make it out alive.

Azula just struck—but not me. I'm okay. She's attacking Zuko! Why are they so bent on attacking each other? Never mind, there's no time now. I have to protect myself.

Actually, I think the only thing keeping me alive this long is their desire to fight with each other—they keep forgetting I'm here! Wow. Azula just blasted Zuko through the wall of an abandoned building! I guess I actually do feel sorry for him. His sister is totally ruthless, and obviously a much more powerful Firebender than he is.

AHHH! I guess since Zuko's still recovering from Azula's blow, she can concentrate on me. I'm trapped in the corner of the blazing building. Stay calm, Aang. Just think—wait, where's that water coming from? It's splashing out the flames! "Katara!" Boy, am I glad to see her. Sokka's here too. Okay, Azula, watch out now. I've got backup.

Azula's holding her own against us. Gosh, she's really powerful.

Wait—why is the ground suddenly rumbling?

"I thought you guys could use a little help," Toph said, sending an Earthbending wave at Azula.

She's back! Boy, am I glad to see her! When this fight is over, I owe her a big apology. And a big thank-you. But first I have to survive this battle.

Just then Zuko's uncle Iroh showed up and helped Zuko to his feet. Then something kind of weird happened. It was like we all realized that Azula was trying to take on the whole world, and that even though we aren't all on the same side of this war, we needed to unite against her. So Katara, Sokka, Toph, Zuko, his uncle, and I formed a circle around Azula.

"I know when I'm beaten," she said. Finally she was surrendering!

But it turned out that she wasn't finished quite yet. She blasted her uncle with a bolt of lightning, and before we could get her back, she vanished. Katara offered to help heal Iroh with her powers, but Zuko refused her help. I can't believe he won't even work with us to help someone he loves. He probably feels humiliated and frustrated by having a sister who's trying to destroy him. But why can't we work together against her? It's strange—for a long time I feared Zuko, and now I kind of pity him.

Sokka, Katara, Toph, and I scrambled onto Appa, and off we flew. Before we settled down for some much-needed sleep, I apologized to Toph and thanked her for coming back.

"Let's see if you still thank me after tomorrow, twinkle toes," Toph said as she slipped into her earth tent. "That's when we begin your Earthbending lessons."

Chapter 5

"Good morning, Earthbending student," Toph said.

I leaped to my feet and snapped to attention. "Good morning, Sifu Toph."

"Hey!" Katara shouted, rubbing the sleep from her eyes. "You never call me Sifu Katara."

Oops! "Well, if you think I should . . . ," I replied, then I turned back to Toph.

"What are you going to teach me first?" I said, barely able to stand still. "Rock-a-lance? Making whirlpools out of land?"

"How about we start with 'move a rock'?" Toph suggested. "The key to Earthbending is your stance," she continued. "You must be steady and strong. Rock is a stubborn element. If you are going to move it, you've got to be firmly rooted—like a rock—yourself."

I watched Toph grip the ground with her toes, as if she were growing right into the earth. Then she swung her arms in a fluid motion and sent a huge boulder flying into the cliff wall. It exploded into a million pieces.

Man, she's good!

"Now you give it a try," Toph said.

I turned toward another boulder and set my feet. Steady, strong, stubborn, I thought. Then I swung my arms toward the boulder.

WHOOSH!

I went flying backward through the air, far away from the boulder I was trying to move. I landed fifty feet away from the thing, and it hadn't even budged!

It's just sitting there mocking me. What did I do wrong? I did exactly what Toph did, I think.

"Maybe if I came at the boulder from another angle, I could—"

"No!" Toph shouted. "That's the problem. Stop thinking like an Airbender. There is no different angle or clever solution or trick that's going to move that rock. You can't dance around the problem like you do with Airbending. You've got to face it head—on. Stay rooted. Be rocklike. I see we've got a lot of work to do."

Stop thinking like an Airbender? How can I do that? It's who I am. Instead of helping me, she's asking me to do the impossible. I didn't have this kind of trouble when Katara taught me Waterbending—I just picked it up immediately. But this is different. And so is Toph. She's not quite as understanding and sweet as Katara.

Next Toph made me run through an obstacle course with a heavy stone on my shoulder. I thought I was going to pass out. Then I had to shove my hands into a barrel of sand. Toph did it easily, but no matter how hard I tried, the sand kept scraping my skin and burning me.

Why is this so hard for me?

Then we tried combat, and I was even worse at that! Toph lunged at me, shouting, "Rock—like!" But I flinched backward, falling back on my old Airbending habits of retreat.

I'm not doing anything right! Maybe I should just quit before I get hurt.

"Stop thinking like an Airbender!" Toph shouted again and again.

I'm trying, but I've approached bending one way my whole life. I can't just force my instincts to change . . . can I?

After hours of practice, I finally made some progress. Toph had me toss a sack of rocks into the air, then move forward and catch it. And I did it! I kept doing it as I moved toward Toph, who was standing across the way. As I neared Toph, she lunged at me. But I stood my ground. I didn't flinch. I didn't jump back. I stayed rooted in my spot like a rock. Toph nodded at me in approval.

I think I might float away, I'm so happy. Of course, that wouldn't be rocklike.

I didn't stay happy for too long. We were at the bottom of a long ramp that Toph had created, and I could see a huge boulder resting at the top of it.

"I'm going to roll that boulder down at you," Toph explained. "If you have the attitude of an Earthbender, you'll stay in your stance and stop the rock."

I suddenly feel sick to my stomach. What happens if I can't do it? Stopping a rolling boulder seems much tougher than simply moving one.

"Sorry, Toph," Katara said, "but are you sure this is really the best way to teach Aang Earthbending?"

"Actually, Katara, there is a better way," Toph said.

Phew! Thank you, Katara! Maybe I won't have to stop that boulder after all. Wait a minute—why is Toph tying a blindfold around my eyes? She can't be serious?

"This way you'll have to sense the vibration of the boulder to stop it," Toph said.

Oh, great! Big help, Katara! Now I'll really get flattened. Okay, just take a deep breath, root your feet to the ground, and set your stance, hands extended in front of you. You are going to stop that boulder, Aang, even with this blindfold on.

Then Toph gave it an Earthbending shove.

Hey, I CAN feel the vibrations through my feet. It's rolling down. I CAN feel the boulder picking up speed. It's close, getting closer, just a few inches away. AHHH! I have to get out of the way! This rock is going to crush me! I just know it. I can't move it! I can't stop it. I'm just not an Earthbender—that's all there is to it! Jump! Jump! Save yourself!

Then the boulder rolled harmlessly past.

"You blew it!" Toph yelled. "You had a perfect stance and perfect form, but when it came
right down to it, you just didn't have the guts!"

She's right. I blew it. What kind of Avatar
am I?

"I know. I'm sorry."

"You ARE sorry. You're a jelly-boned wimp.
Now, do you have what it takes to face that
rock like an Earthbender?"

Why does she have to yell at me all the
time? Why does she have to make everything
so hard? She treats me like I'm a little kid, and
like she's the greatest thing that ever lived. I
can't stand it anymore.

"No," I replied, turning away. "I don't think I
have what it takes."

⊕ ⊕ ⊕

Katara suggested that we work on some Waterbending. I honestly don't feel like doing much of
anything. But Katara's being so nice to me, and
working on some Waterbending might lift my
spirits. Anything to get away from my failure for
a little while. Anything to forget how much I stink
at Earthbending, and how mean Toph is.

"You know this block you're having is only

temporary, right?" Katara said.

I knew she couldn't go long without bringing it up.

"I don't want to talk about it."

"That's the problem, Aang. If you face this issue instead of avoiding it, that's the Earthbender way."

"I know! I get it, all right? I need to face it head-on, like a rock. Be rocklike. I know. But I just can't do it. I don't know why I can't, but I can't."

I wish everyone would just leave me alone! But of course, she won't.

"Aang, if fire and water are opposites, then what's the opposite of air?"

"I guess it's earth."

"That's why it's so hard for you to get this. You're working with your natural opposite. But you'll figure it out. I know you will."

I never actually thought about it that way. But it seems to make sense. Maybe the key to getting Earthbending is to think and do the opposite of what I've always done as an Airbender. Could it be as simple as that? I think I can do that. At least I can try again.

Just when I started feeling better, Toph started acting up. First she took some nuts from my bag without asking. I really didn't mind that—I'm always happy to share. But then she started using my antique staff, which was handcrafted by the monks, as a nutcracker. That kind of bothered me.

I think she's intentionally trying to make me mad. She probably thinks it will trigger some deep well of Earthbending power or something. Thing is, I'm not really mad. Sharing is just part of who I am. But I might ask her to leave my staff alone. Maybe later—I'm not ready for another confrontation with her right now.

Just then Katara came to tell me that she couldn't find Sokka. We split up to search and I found him stuck in a hole in the ground. I tried to Airbend him out, but all I ended up doing was blowing dust in his face.

"Aang, I know you're new at it," Sokka said, "but I could use a little Earthbending here!"

I just can't. What if I try and fail again? I'd feel like an even bigger loser. I suppose I could go get Toph, but that would be like admitting I'm a great big failure.

Just then an angry saber—toothed moose

lioness came looking for her cub, which Sokka had been playing with before he fell in the hole.

"Aang, this is bad!" Sokka said, panicking. "You've got to get me out of here!"

Okay, this is serious. Sokka's life is at stake. I have to stop feeling sorry for myself and just do what Toph's been telling me. It's time to start thinking like an Earthbender and get Sokka out of there!

My feet are planted. I am not about to move, no matter what, not even now that the beast is charging right at me. Wait—she's stopping! She's turning around and walking away. Did I make her leave? Was my will so rocklike that she couldn't stand up to me?

Then Toph jumped out from behind the bushes.

She's been watching the whole time? "Why didn't you help us?" I asked. I can't believe she put us both in such danger.

"Guess it just didn't occur to me," she said as she dropped a nut onto the ground and went to smash it with my staff.

That does it. Now I AM mad. That staff is important to me and she has no right to treat it that way. "Enough!" I reached out and grabbed the staff before it struck the ground. "I want my staff back. Now!"

"Do it!" Toph shouted, letting go of the staff. "Do it now!"

"Do what?"

"Earthbend, twinkle toes! You just stood your ground against a crazed beast, and even more impressive, you stood your ground against me. You've got the stuff! Now do it!"

As bossy as she was being, I knew she was probably right. So I set my feet and focused my mind. Then I whipped my arms around in an Earthbending move and sent a bunch of big rocks flying.

"You did it!" Toph cried. "You're an Earth-bender!"

She's proud of me! Actually, I'm kind of proud of myself. I can't believe I did it. I AM an Earthbender. I turned to set Sokka free with an Earthbending move, but Toph stopped me.

"You should probably let me do that. You're still a little new to this and you might acciden-tally crush him."

Chapter 6

Today we met this professor of anthropology who was looking for this legendary library. It's supposed to have more books than any other in the world. Sokka thought that it might have a map of the Fire Nation, or just some information that would be helpful. So we decided to go with him to find the library. When we found the library, Sokka, Katara, the professor, Momo, and I went inside while Toph waited outside with Appa.

Inside, Sokka made an amazing discovery— Firebenders lose their power during a solar eclipse because the sun is covered up! Then we were able to calculate the date of the next solar eclipse using this incredible calendar.

"If we attack the Fire Nation on that date, they'll be helpless," cried Sokka. "We've got to get this info to the Earth King at Ba Sing Se!"

Unfortunately the spirit of the library overheard Sokka, and he was so angry that we were using his knowledge for our own purposes that he decided to sink the library into the desert to keep its knowledge from humans.

The professor decided to stay, surrounded by all the world's knowledge, but thankfully Sokka, Katara, and I got out just as the library disappeared into the sand.

We're finally outside. Phew! But the strange thing is, I can't see Appa anywhere. There's Toph. . . . Where could he have gone? And why does Toph look so serious?

"Where's Appa?" She's not responding. . . . That's a bad sign.

"Toph, what happened?" Oh, no! I have this horrible sinking feeling rising from the pit of my stomach. "Where's Appa?"

I listened in horror as Toph told me that when

the library started sinking, she used all her Earth-bending abilities to hold it up until we got out. While she was doing that, a group of Sandbenders kidnapped Appa and took him away.

I feel like a piece of my own body has just been ripped out. I can't remember a time in my life when Appa wasn't by my side. And now he's gone! Gone!

"How could you let them take Appa!" I don't care if she's my Earthbending teacher. I just want Appa back! "Why didn't you stop them?"

"I couldn't," she replied weakly. "The library was sinking, and you guys were still inside. I would have lost all of you if I stopped to save Appa. I can hardly feel any vibrations out here in the sand. The Sandbenders snuck up on me and I didn't have time to—"

"You just didn't care! You never liked Appa! You wanted him gone!"

Enough excuses! I can't believe this—what if I never get him back?

Then Katara stepped between us. "Aang, stop it! You know Toph did all she could. She saved our lives!"

Now Katara's turned against me! This is just

too much. "That's all any of you guys care about—yourselves! You don't care if Appa is okay!"

I've never felt more alone. My lifelong buddy is gone. My friends have all turned on me. It's obvious I'm not going to get any help. I'm going to have to find Appa myself.

"I'm going after Appa." I whipped open my glider. Then I turned to Toph. "Which direction did they go?"

Toph shrugged and pointed. I looked at the ground and saw a trail left by the sand sailer the Sandbenders must have been riding.

"I'll be back when I find him." Then I leaped into the sky.

I'm so upset, I could cry. I don't know what I'll do if he's really gone. How can your best friend in the whole world be there one second and then just be gone the next? It doesn't make any sense. Come on, Aang. Keep looking. Find him!

I followed the tracks for a little while, but soon they were wiped away by the desert winds. I flew over the desert for hours, searching in every direction, but it was no use.

I glided to a landing back where the library was, and Katara came over and placed her hand on my shoulder. "I'm sorry, Aang. I know it's hard for you right now, but we need to focus on getting out of here."

I don't feel like focusing on anything but Appa. Nothing matters at all. Not my friends, not being the Avatar, not saving the world. Not even getting out of this desert alive. "What's the difference? We won't survive without Appa. We all know it."

Katara kept trying to cheer me up, but I was barely listening. People call me the last Airbender, but that's not really true. Appa was—is—an Airbender too. Nobody, not even Katara, understands him the way I do. To everyone else he's just a big furry animal. But I know that he's a special being, as close to me as any of my human friends.

Suddenly Katara grabbed my hand and pulled me up to my feet.

"Aang, get up. We're getting out of this desert."

She seems really adamant about leaving. I really don't care either way. Without Appa, nothing matters.

Katara decided that it would be better if we rested during the day and traveled at night, using the stars to navigate our way to Ba Sing Se. As we walked, Toph stubbed her toes on something in the sand. It turned out to be a sand sailer.

"It's got a compass on it," Katara said excitedly. "Aang, if you can bend a breeze, we can sail to Ba Sing Se. We're going to make it!"

I felt a little better that we weren't all going to die out there. But not much. I used my Airbending to power the sail and we glided across the desert until all of a sudden, we were attacked by buzzard—wasps. Then, out of nowhere, a huge sandstorm rose up, blow—ing the creatures away. When the storm died down, we saw that a group of Sandbenders had whipped up the storm to save us.

But I'm in no mood to say thanks. It was Sandbenders who took Appa. . . .

"What are you doing in our land with what looks like a stolen sand sailer?" the leader of the Sandbenders demanded.

"We're traveling with the Avatar. Our bison was stolen and we have to get to Ba Sing Se," Katara replied. "We found the sailer aban—doned in the desert."

"You dare accuse our people of theft when you ride in a stolen sand sailer?" yelled a younger Sandbender angrily.

"Quiet, Ghashiun!" an older man shouted. "No one accused our people of anything!"

"Sorry, Father," Ghashiun said, stepping back.

Toph leaned in close to me. "I recognize the son's voice, and I never forget a voice," she whispered. "He's the one who stole Appa."

I rushed toward Ghashiun, my anger rising quickly. "You stole Appa!" I shouted, boiling with rage. "Where is he? What did you do to him?"

"They're lying!" Ghashiun cried. "They're the thieves!"

These people are going to tell me where Appa is or pay a heavy price! I'll show them how serious I am with a massive Airbending blast to one of their sand sailers—

BAM!

It shattered into splinters. The Sandbenders backed away, stunned.

"Where is my bison?"

"It wasn't me!" Ghashiun cried.

"You said to put a muzzle on him!" Toph shouted.

"You muzzled Appa?!" I can barely control myself. The thought of it makes me want to scream!

I fired an Airbending blast at another sand sailer, then turned my sights on the Sandbenders themselves. Usually the thought of fighting another person is against everything I believe in, against everything the monks taught me. I'm sorry, but I can't control myself from using force against these people. . . .

"I'm sorry!" Ghashiun cried. "I didn't know it belonged to the Avatar!"

"Tell me where Appa is!"

"I traded him to some nomads. He's probably in Ba Sing Se by now. They were going to sell him there."

Appa for sale, like some piece of meat? I can't take it anymore. I'm so angry, I could . . . I could . . .

My anger overcame me and I slipped into the Avatar state. After a while, I felt a strange calm wash over me as I left my body and rose above the desert floor. Looking down, I could see that my wrath had stirred up vicious desert winds whipping everyone below. I saw Sokka grab Toph and pull her away from me. I saw the Sandbenders running from me in terror. Then I saw my body standing in the center of the whirlwind.

But Katara, fighting the wind with each step, slowly made her way toward me. She didn't seem afraid of me this time. She just took hold of my body and hugged me. She didn't say a word.

Gradually my anger subsided and I saw the winds die down. Then I felt myself returning to earth, to my body. Katara did something for me that words could not do. The simple act of hugging me told me that she was there for me completely, without judgment, without lectures, without fear. It struck a chord deep inside me. I felt my heart open up to her. . . .

Then the wind stopped. But the pain I'd been keeping at bay rushed in with the force of a hurricane. I closed my eyes, gave myself over to Katara's arms, and cried harder than I had ever cried in my life.

Chapter 7

I did my best to push Appa out of my mind. I tried to focus all my thoughts and energy on getting to Ba Sing Se to tell the Earth King about the solar eclipse.

We finally got out of the desert and arrived at a waterfall pond. We ended up traveling across this stretch of land called Serpent's Pass, along with a refugee family that we met on the way. Serpent's Pass was definitely scary, but we made it through safely.

Katara keeps asking me about Appa, and I want to talk about it, but after what happened back in the desert, I'm trying to stay as unemotional as possible. The Avatar state is really dangerous, and until I know how to control it, I'd rather not get angry or upset enough to go into it again. I guess it's hard for Katara to understand that, though. She's all about feelings, and stuff like that.

Did I mention that one of the members of the refugee family is pregnant? Well, she just went into labor. It's pretty lucky we're off Serpent's Pass, huh? Katara has taken charge and is delivering the baby now; she used to help Gran Gran deliver babies back home. Wait, I just heard crying . . . it's a boy!

Now I'm inside the tent. There are the mom and dad, cuddling their newborn son. The baby is the most beautiful thing I've ever seen! It's amazing to watch them celebrate in the midst of all this pain and fighting, but I think the new life came to remind us that life goes on no mat—ter what. I guess this is what living is all about: loving and caring for your family.

Sometimes I forget that I have a family now too—Katara, Sokka, Momo, and Appa. Even Toph. Just because Appa is missing, that doesn't mean I should stop caring about every—one else I love in my life. In fact, losing Appa has actually made me realize that I should show them how much I care about them, because we never know what might happen. It's okay for me to miss Appa. It's okay for me to feel sad, and to lean on Katara for help. That's what family is for, right?

"I've been going through a really hard time lately," I told the family. "But you've made me hopeful again."

Katara took my hand and smiled sweetly. My heart is beating so fast I can hardly breathe! "I thought I was trying to be strong, Katara. But I was really just running away from my feelings. Seeing this family together, so full of happiness and love, reminded me of how I feel about Appa."

Come on Aang, you can do it. . . .

"And how I feel about you." That's what I should have said in the Cave of Two Lovers. . . . Oh well, I hope I've at least redeemed myself from that!

Katara burst into tears. I guess I really do have a family. A pretty good one, too, if you ask me!

I said good—bye, then Momo and I took off to find Appa. "I promise, I'll find Appa as fast as I can. I just really need to do this. I'll see you all in Ba Sing Se."

Chapter 8

We're almost at the outer wall of Ba Sing Se. I can't wait to find Appa! Wait, what's that? Oh, no! A huge Fire Nation invasion force is marching toward the city! There must be thousands of tanks and troops advancing toward the outer wall. And what's that? Some kind of huge metal drill? This can only mean one thing: They're planning on drilling right through the outer wall of Ba Sing Se to invade the city. This is awful! I have to warn the others!

"Sorry, Momo. Appa's going to have to wait."

I met my friends right outside Ba Sing Se's outer wall and told them about the drill. Toph and

I Earthbended a ledge of rock up the side of the outer wall so that everyone could climb up and see the scary-looking drill moving closer and closer.

Once inside the gates, I marched up to the first guard I could find. I told him that I was the Avatar and he should take me to whoever was in charge. Then the three Firebenders who were following us showed up and attacked the Earth Kingdom soldiers. One of them, Ty Lee, actually takes people's chi away, leaving them unable to bend. Pretty scary stuff.

Anyway, Sokka has a plan to stop the drill by hitting its pressure points. The drill is made up of an inner section and an outer one. We figure if we cut through the braces, the whole thing will collapse.

As we walked back toward the drill, Toph whipped up a dust storm so that we wouldn't be seen. When the drill was directly above us, Sokka, Katara, Momo, and I jumped onto it. Toph stayed outside to slow the drill down from there with her Earthbending.

🪙 🪙 🪙

We're making our way through the drill; it's a twisting maze of pipes and valves. It's turning out to be too hard to cut through them completely, so we're just going to weaken them, and then I'll go up to the top of the drill and deliver a final Air-bending blow. Then the whole thing will collapse!

It sounds simple enough, but the thing is, everyone inside the city is depending on this plan succeeding. Once again, it's all up to me, the Avatar. I just hope that I won't let them down. . . .

🌐 🌐 🌐

One by one we hurried from brace to brace, slashing each one with our waterwhips until it was weakened. Just as we were finishing with the final brace, the three firebenders—Azula, Mai, and Ty Lee—launched an attack on us.

"Split up!" I cried. Katara tossed me her water pouch, then she and Sokka dashed down a corridor. Ty Lee and Mai followed them. Azula stayed behind.

"The Avatar's mine!" she cried.

I don't have time for this now—I have to complete our plan! Momo and I are dashing through the tank—we're finally at the top. Oh, no! The drill is already boring into the outer wall—the last line of the Earth Kingdom's defense!

I used Katara's water to slash an X-shaped

cut into the top of the drill's armor in prepa-
ration for my final blow. That's when Azula
caught up with me and unleashed blast after
blast of fire. I deflected what I could by Airbending, but when I tried to stop her with a
water whip, she evaporated my supply! No
matter what I did, she had me backing up.

Is Azula just too powerful for me to defeat? I
actually feel sorry for Zuko now, having to deal
with such a ruthless enemy, not to mention sister!
Zuko is dangerous, but at least he has a decent
reason for always trying to capture me: to get back
into the good graces of his father, the Fire Lord.
Azula is just plain crazy. It's like she enjoys hurting people and destroying things—as if she finds
that fun, not just a necessary part of war. That
ruthlessness makes her a much more dangerous
opponent than Zuko ever could be. I'd take Zuko
over his cold-blooded sister any day.

Azula keeps firing at me. I just need to keep
fighting. . . . Azula may be more powerful than
me, but I have to be smarter. I HAVE to stop her
so I can bring down the drill.

Yes! She stumbled. Now's my chance . . .

While Azula struggled to regain her balance,

I grabbed a big rock. I Earthbended the rock in half, sharpening one end into a point. Then I rested the point in the X—shaped cut. I just needed some momentum for this to work. . . .

Just as Azula got back to her feet, I dashed down the wall, leaped into the air, and came down with all my might. Using a powerful Earthbending blow, I slammed my hands into the top of the rock spike I had made and left on top of the X—shaped cut in the drill.

BOOM!

The spike dug into the hull with such force that the weakened braces split and the whole machine broke apart. A river of slurry shot from the hole I had created, knocking Azula off the machine. I hopped onto the slurry and rode the wave down, like a surfer.

Woohoo! This is so great! The drill has been destroyed, the Fire Nation attack has been stopped, and the city is safe.

I almost feel free again, like I used to feel all the time when I went penguin sledding, and riding giant porpoises just for fun—before this war started, before Azula. I kind of feel like I'm just Aang again, not Aang the Avatar.

Chapter 9

In order to travel from the outer wall into the city, we rode a train along a monorail. When we got off at the Ba Sing Se train station, we stepped out onto a busy platform. My thoughts drifted back to Appa. I'd been so caught up in getting to Ba Sing Se, then in stopping the Fire Nation attack and destroying the drill, that I didn't allow myself time to think about my buddy. But we're here now, where he's been taken, and I promise I'm NOT going to leave this city without him.

At the station a woman came up to us and introduced herself as Joo Dee. She already knew who we were. She said it was her job to show us around the city, and so off we went in a fancy carriage pulled by a team of ostrich horses. As we rode, Sokka tried to explain to Joo Dee that we had important information for the king about the Fire Nation. But each time he brought it up, she changed the subject or ignored him.

"You're in Ba Sing Se now," she said. "Everyone is safe here."

Actually, before I got here Ba Sing Se was about to be invaded by the Fire Nation and their giant drill, but she just won't listen. Ba Sing Se is turning out to be a really strange city. There are three different sections: the lower, middle, and upper rings. They are divided by classes; the poorest people live in the lower ring and the richest live in the upper. I don't think I'm comfort—able with that. I mean, I grew up listening to the monks teaching about equality and sharing.

Anyway, Joo Dee brought us to the upper ring. She pointed out the king's royal palace, and the Dai Li agents around it. Apparently the Dai Li is the cultural authority of the city. Then she showed us our new house. I wasn't planning on staying here long, but she said we have to wait a month before our appointment with the king!

We decided we'd spend the time looking for Appa. We had hoped that Joo Dee would leave us alone, but she insisted on escorting us all over. It didn't matter anyway; we didn't get very far.

I had such a strong feeling that Appa was there, but nobody we asked seemed to be able to help us find him!

After a totally frustrating day, Joo Dee finally dropped us off at our house. We met our next—door neighbor, Pong, hoping maybe we could get some answers from him. He was friendly enough, but as soon as we mentioned the war, he began trembling and looking around to see if he was being watched.

"Listen," he said, obviously frightened. "You can't mention the war in Ba Sing Se. And whatever you do, stay away from the Dai Li." Then he ran into his house and slammed the door behind him.

No one in this city will talk about anything important. It seems like some kind of conspiracy or something.

"We have to see the Earth King," Sokka insisted. "That's the only way to straighten this out."

Sokka's right. The king HAS to help us. I'm sure of it. And I'm NOT waiting a whole month in this weird city to see him!

A little while later, Katara was reading the paper and discovered that the king was having a party. She suggested that we sneak in and try to talk to him there. So she and Toph get to dress up like fancy society ladies, while Sokka and I have to pretend that we're busboys. The things I have to do sometimes!

We snuck in and spotted the Earth King, but on our way to him we were caught by Dai Li agents and taken to a library inside the palace. Then this guy approached me. He said his name was Long Feng, and that he was the grand secretariat of Ba Sing Se, cultural minister to the king, and head of the Dai Li. I asked him why he wouldn't let us see the king, and told him about the Fire Nation drill and the solar eclipse, but he didn't seem to care! He just said that the king had no time to get involved with politics or military activities, which makes no sense! What else does the king DO? All that stuff is his job. ESPECIALLY during a war. He said that silencing talk of the conflict made Ba Sing Se a peaceful, orderly utopia. Talk about crazy—this guy's nuttier than General Fong for sure!

Unfortunately, yelling at Long Feng just made him angrier at me. He told me he knew I was looking for Appa, and made it seem like he had the power to help, or to make it impossible. . . . Does he know where Appa is? I think Long Feng knows a lot more than he lets on. I need to find out what this guy is hiding, but it's going to take a little bit of planning. Right now, I just have to be calm.

And now there's this strange woman who wants to escort us home.

"What happened to Joo Dee?" Katara asked.

"I'm Joo Dee," the woman said, smiling. "I'll be your host as long as you're in our wonderful city!"

Just when I thought things couldn't get any stranger. What in the world is going on in this crazy city?

Chapter 10

My mind is racing and I can't slow it down. I'm trying really hard to figure out the next step to take so that we can find Appa. I'm trying to understand why nobody in this city wants to talk about a war that's on the verge of destroying their home—and the rest of the world! What is with these people?

Katara, Sokka, Toph, and I decided to go put up MISSING BISON posters all around the city, in the hopes that maybe someone had seen Appa somewhere. When we got back home, someone knocked on the front door. I was certain it would be someone with good news about Appa. But to my disappointment, it was only Joo Dee—the first Joo Dee— holding one of our posters. When we asked her where she had been, she told us that she took a short vacation at a place called Lake Laogai. Weird! Then she told us that we were forbidden to put up posters.

What CAN you do in this city? Anyway, I'm done listening to these people. It's obvious they don't want to help us, so we'll just help ourselves.

"We don't care about the rules, and we're not asking permission. We're finding Appa on our own, and you should just stay out of our way!" I slammed the door in her face. "From now on we do whatever it takes to find Appa."

We headed out of the house, more deter- mined than ever. Then—I couldn't believe it—Katara ran into Jet, this rebel we had met earlier in our travels. What's he doing in Ba Sing Se? Now that I think back on it, Katara kind of had a crush on Jet—until he put a whole innocent village in danger trying to fight the Fire Nation! That's when Katara decided that she wanted nothing to do with him. I don't mind that part at all.

"I'm here to help you find Appa," said Jet.

He told Katara that he had changed, that he had given up his gang. I know she doesn't trust him, but at this point I really need all the help that I can get.

Jet led us to a warehouse where he had heard Appa had been taken. But when we got there, it was empty. At first Katara thought it was a trap, but then we found some of Appa's fur on the ground.

"They took that big thing yesterday," said a voice from a dark corner of the building. A janitor pushing a broom stepped into the light. "Some rich guy on Whaletail Island bought him—maybe for a zoo, or maybe for the meat."

FOR THE MEAT! I have to sit down. This feeling in my stomach is not good. . . . The idea of someone buying Appa for meat made me nauseous and furious at the same time. Appa is the last of a noble, proud breed, not somebody's dinner. I wasn't going to let anything happen to him! "We've got to get to Whaletail Island right away!"

Sokka looked it up on his map and discovered that it was really far away, back near the

South Pole. But I don't care how far away it is or how long it takes to get there. If there's a chance to find Appa, we have to take it.

On our way out of the warehouse, we ran into the members of Jet's gang, who told us that Jet had been arrested and dragged away by the Dai Li a few weeks earlier. Jet denied it and looked at them like they were crazy. He also denied being part of the gang altogether. Toph is kind of like a human lie detector, and she studied their heartbeats and breathing patterns and told us that both Jet and his gang friends were telling the truth.

"They both THINK they're telling the truth," Sokka realized suddenly. "That's because Jet's been brainwashed by the Dai Li!"

We grabbed Jet and brought him back to his apartment, where we tried to jog his memory.

"The Dai Li must have sent Jet and that janitor to mislead us," Katara said.

That made perfect sense! They wanted us out of Ba Sing Se, because we were stirring up trouble with our talk about the war, so they brainwashed Jet to lead us far away.

"I bet they still have Appa right here in the city!" I said, feeling hopeful again. "Maybe he's in the same place they took Jet!" I leaned in close to Jet. "Where did they take you?"

"Nowhere!" he cried, squirming in his chair. "I don't know what you're talking about!"

Katara used the water from her pouch and formed a sparkling band of healing energy around Jet's head to jog his memory. Slowly he began to relax.

"They took me to Dai Li headquarters," he said finally. "It was underwater, under a lake."

"Joo Dee said she went on a vacation to Lake Laogai," Sokka recalled.

"That's it!" Jet cried. "Lake Laogai!"

I'm certain now that's where we'll find Appa. I hope that we won't be too late. I don't know what I'll do if—NO, Aang, don't think that way! We WILL find Appa, and he'll be all right.

Sokka, Katara, Toph, Momo, and I traveled to Lake Laogai, along with Jet and two members of his gang, Longshot and Smellerbee. It was a big, beautiful lake surrounded by a thick woods. But there was no sign of a head—

quarters or any kind of passageway leading under the water.

Then Toph found a rock hatch in the water at the edge of the shore. She Earthbended the hatch open and revealed a stairway leading down under the lake. We hurried down the stairs and into a tunnel.

"It's coming back to me now," Jet said. "I think there's a cell big enough to hold Appa just ahead."

We're so close now. He might even be right around the next bend!

We made our way along the tunnel, which had rooms and holding cells on either side. In one of the rooms I saw a bunch of women all being trained—brainwashed, actually—to be Joo Dees. It was so creepy, like they were all preprogrammed robots. Yuck!

Continuing along the tunnel, we soon came to a door where Jet stopped. "I think it's through here," he said, flinging open the door.

Wait a second—this isn't Appa's cell. It's a room filled with Dai Li agents. There's Long Feng! Did Jet lead us into a trap, or did he just make an honest mistake?

"By breaking into our headquarters you have made yourselves enemies of the state," Long Feng announced. Then he turned to his agents. "Take them into custody!"

The Dai Li agents attacked, but we fought back. Then Long Feng started running, and Jet and I took off after him. We followed him back down the tunnel and into another room, where he slammed the door and turned to confront us. Jet is definitely on our side.

"All right, Avatar," Long Feng snarled confidently. "This is your last chance—if you want your bison back."

He does have Appa! I knew it! I could strike him down right where he stands, but not before I learn where he's holding my buddy.

"Tell me where Appa is!"

"Agree to exit the city now, and I'll waive all charges and allow you to leave with your lost pet," Long Feng said.

"You're in no position to bargain!" Jet shouted, drawing his twin hook swords.

"Definitely not," I added, taking up a combat stance beside Jet. If Long Feng wants to do this the hard way, I'll gladly accommodate him.

Then he looked Jet right in the eye and said, "Jet, the Earth King has invited you to Lake Laogai."

Jet's expression is completely changing—his eyes are narrower, and he's staring blankly ahead. What's happening to him?

"I am honored to accept his invitation," Jet said in a flat emotionless voice.

Long Feng just said the phrase that triggers Jet's brainwashing! This is not good!

A second later Jet attacked me, and Long Feng ran toward the door. I tried to stop Jet without hurting him, while doing my best to avoid the pointy tips of his swords.

"Jet, it's me, Aang. I'm your friend! You don't need to do this!"

Uh-oh, I'm not getting through to him! He just keeps lunging at me with his swords, and I can't keep dodging them forever. . . .

"Jet, look inside your heart. He can't make you do this—you're a freedom fighter!"

Wait! I think I may have just jogged his memory. He's stopped attacking me and he's just standing there staring . . . and now he's attacking Long Feng! Finally we're making progress!

I was about to help Jet fight Long Feng, but everything happened so fast, and before I knew it, Long Feng had blasted Jet with an Earthbending move that took him to the ground. Then Long Feng Earthbended himself out of the cave, and the whole gang rushed into the cave to find Jet hurt and lying on the ground. Katara tried to heal him, but Smellerbee and Longshot told us to go find Appa. They vowed to take care of him. Katara looked so upset, and even though Jet promised her he'd be all right, I wonder if he will be. We had to get to

Appa before Long Feng did, so we left them and rushed down the tunnel until we came to a big holding cell. But we were too late. It was empty. Broken chains dangled from the wall. Appa's fur was everywhere.

"He's gone! Long Feng beat us here!" Again, I was too late. He'd been right here and I'd missed him.

"Maybe we can catch them," Sokka said, urging us on.

We raced back up the stairs and out of the headquarters. Back on the lake's shore we were surrounded by Dai Li troops.

It's over. We failed. I'm sorry, buddy. I let you down.

Just then, Momo started screeching like crazy and took off into the sky. When I looked up to see where he was going, I saw the most beautiful sight I'd ever seen. There, swooping majestically through the sky, is Appa.

He's alive! He's safe! He's free! He hasn't become somebody's pet or slave or dinner. Here's my buddy, back again at last. I'm so happy, I could cry!

"Appa!" I yelled.

Appa's reply came in the form of a huge Airbending blast that flattened the Dai Li troops. It turned out that when Long Feng had tried to take on Appa, Appa bit him on the leg and tossed him into the lake.

That's my buddy!

I leaped into the sky and landed on Appa's neck, hugging him with all my might. When my friends were all aboard, I shouted, "Yip, yip!" for the first time in weeks, and we took off into the sky.

"I missed you, buddy, more than you'll ever know."

Chapter 11

We finally made it inside the palace and into the throne room of the Earth King.

"We need to talk to you!" I said to the king. Then I spotted Long Feng standing at the king's side.

Great. I thought we got rid of this guy.

"He's lying!" Long Feng shouted. "They're here to overthrow you!"

Long Feng had convinced the king we were his enemies. But I told the king that I was the Avatar and he agreed to listen to me. I explained about the war and that the Dai Li had kept it secret from him in order to control the city and to control him.

"Long Feng didn't want us to tell you about all this, so he stole our sky bison to blackmail us," I explained. Now that I was finally with the king, I wasn't going to let anything stop me from telling him the truth.

Long Feng denied ever having seen a sky bison, so I Airbended his robe up to show Appa's teeth marks in his leg. Long Feng claimed it was just a birthmark, but Sokka brought Appa into the throne room and showed off his teeth.

"That pretty much proves it," the king said. "But it doesn't prove this crazy conspiracy theory," the king added.

What's it going to take to convince him that his entire kingdom is in danger?

"I suppose this matter is worth looking into," the king then said.

He agreed to come with us to give us a chance to prove that we were telling the truth. We took him to Lake Laogai to expose the Dai Li's secret headquarters, but when we got there, all evidence of the headquarters was gone. The Dai Li had already destroyed the evidence. The king was ready to return home, but then Katara had a brilliant idea.

"The wall!" she cried. "And the drill. They'll never be able to cover that up in time!"

We flew back to the city and Appa landed on top of the outer wall. The drill still stuck out of the wall, right where we stopped it.

"What is that?" the king asked anxiously.

"It's a giant drill made by the Fire Nation to break through your walls," Sokka explained.

This was proof that we were telling the truth. Now the king finally knew that the war was real.

"I can't believe I never knew," the king said.

"I can explain this, Your Majesty," said a voice approaching us. It was Long Feng.

This ought to be good.

"This is nothing more than a construction project," he said, though it sounded as if even he had trouble believing it.

"Really?" said Katara. "Then perhaps you could explain why there's a Fire Nation insignia on your construction equipment."

I love Katara! I mean, whoa, I can't believe I admitted that, even if it is just in my own head. But I really do. I mean, she's so clever! She just backed Long Feng into a corner, and now we definitely have him right where we want him.

General Sung joined us on the wall and told the king that we were heroes.

"Without them," the general said, "our city would have been lost to the Fire Nation army."

The king ordered the Dai Li to arrest Long Feng. "He will stand trial for crimes against the Earth Kingdom," the king announced. Then the Dai Li hauled Long Feng away.

Back in the throne room, we filled in the king on the approaching comet, which would make the Fire Nation too powerful to stop, and the solar eclipse during which the Earth Kingdom army must attack the Fire Nation, which would be at its weakest. He agreed to attack on the day of the eclipse—the Day of Black Sun.

We did it! I'm so excited, I can hardly stand it! We found Appa, we saved the Earth Kingdom from the Fire Nation drill, and we delivered information to the king that can save the whole world. Sometimes it's really good being the Avatar.

Just then the door swung open and General How, leader of the council of generals, entered the throne room. He said that they'd found some things in Long Feng's office that were for us. He handed Toph a letter from her mother. Katara read it and reported that Toph's mom said she was in Ba Sing Se and wanted to see Toph.

Then he handed me a scroll.

"This scroll was attached to the horn of your bison when the Dai Li captured him," the general said.

"I can't believe it," I said after reading the note. "There's a man living at the Eastern Air Temple. A guru. A kind of spiritual expert who says he can help me take the next step in my Avatar journey."

Then he handed Katara an intelligence report that said her father was with a small fleet of Water Tribe ships at Chameleon Bay.

"I hate to say it," Katara began, "but we have to split up."

We just found Appa, and now Katara wants us to separate? I don't want to let any of them out of my sight—ever again.

"You have to meet this guru, Aang," she said. "If we're going to invade the Fire Nation, you need to be ready."

It's times like these when I wish I were just plain Aang again so that the fate of the world didn't always depend on me fulfilling my destiny. But I have no choice. She's right. I have to go.

Then Sokka pointed out that one of us had to stay there with the king and help him plan the invasion. He volunteered, but sweet, self-less Katara said that she would stay so that Sokka could go see their father.

She's the absolute best. Always putting others' needs before hers. I'm totally and completely crazy about her! There's no other way to put it. Now I just really need to tell her how I feel.

We all prepared to go our separate ways, then met up to say good-bye. I needed a moment alone with Katara, so I pulled her away from the group.

"Katara, I need to tell you something. I've been wanting to say it for a long time." Oh, boy. I'm so nervous I can hardly breathe. Here we go. . . .

"What is it, Aang?" she asked.

I've rehearsed this speech a thousand times in my head, but now that the moment is here to actually say it aloud, I don't even know where to begin. I looked up into Katara's beautiful eyes and I just blurted out—

"Katara, I—"

"All right!" Sokka shouted, punching me playfully in the stomach. "Who's ready to get going on a little men-only man trip!"

I can't believe this! Can't he see we're in the middle of something? Now the moment's gone, shattered, lost. Thanks a lot, Sokka. I was so close. . . .

Just then, a messenger arrived to tell the king that three female warriors from the island of Kyoshi were here to see him.

"That's Suki!" Sokka cried. "She'll be here when we get back." Did I mention Sokka has a crush on Suki?

Katara, Toph, Sokka, and I stood in a circle, huddling together. Then Katara hugged me and kissed me sweetly on the head. The head's not exactly the lips, but it's a start, isn't it?

Finally, Sokka and I climbed onto Appa and off we flew. All I can think about is Katara. I miss her already and can't wait to see her face again. And from the look on Sokka's face, he's thinking about Suki.

"I can't believe I'm saying this," Sokka said. "But things are finally looking up for us."

降去神

Chapter 12

I dropped Sokka off, and Appa and I kept going
till we reached the Eastern Air Temple. As we
descended through the mist at sunset, I spotted
a small man sitting and meditating among the
overgrown gardens and ruined buildings.

He told me he was Guru Pathik, and that
he could teach me how to control the Avatar
state. He also said he knew my old teacher,
Monk Gyatso. That's all I needed to hear. I
was totally ready to learn from this guy.

Guru Pathik took me to a cave deep inside
a mountain and we began. He started out by
explaining that controlling the Avatar state

involves finding a balance between the mind, spirit, and body. Then he explained that energy flows through the body like water in a stream, and that the body contains seven chakras. These are pools of spiraling energy. When the chakras get blocked, the energy can't flow and my power as the Avatar is weakened.

So my job is to open my seven chakras. Doesn't sound too tough!

"First we will open the Earth Chakra. It deals with survival and is blocked by fear," Guru Pathik explained.

"What are you most afraid of?" he asked. "Let your fears become clear to you."

I closed my eyes and began meditating. Visions and memories rushed into my mind—the Blue Spirit attacking me with swords, Katara being buried in rock by General Fong—and then, suddenly, Guru Pathik was gone and the Fire Lord himself was right in front of me! He filled the cave with flames.

I've failed on my first attempt! And I'm responsible for bringing the Fire Lord here to destroy the sacred temple, to kill Guru Pathik.

Then a calm voice cut through my panic

and fear. "Aang, your vision is not real."

I opened my eyes and saw Guru Pathik. No Fire Lord. No flames. It was all in my head. My hands shook and sweat poured down my face.

"You fear for your survival, but you must sur— render these fears. Your spirit can never die."

"But Roku told me that if I'm killed in the Avatar state, the Avatar cycle will end!"

"Once your chakras are clear, you'll be able to control the Avatar state so that you won't need to worry about that."

Well, that makes me feel a whole lot better! Since Roku told me about the Avatar spirit, I've lived in fear of the Avatar state. I don't want to be the one to end the Avatar spirit's cycle. But since I won't have to worry about that anymore, let's try this again.

I closed my eyes and the Fire Lord stood before me.

"Let your fears flow down the creek," Guru Pathik said softly.

I don't fear you, Fire Lord. In fact, soon YOU'RE going to have to fear me. So go away. Get out of my head!

Wow! It worked. The flames in the cave are

flickering out, and the Fire Lord is vanishing into the shadows on the walls.

"You have opened your Earth Chakra."

Next came the Water Chakra, which deals with pleasure and is blocked by guilt. Again I began to meditate.

"Look at all the guilt which burdens you. What do you blame yourself for?"

My mind flooded with images of me running away from the Air Nomads when I should have stayed to complete my studies; of me screaming at Toph, blaming her when Appa was taken; and then, most powerful of all, of everyone I hurt and scared when I was out of control in the Avatar state. I hurt so many people. I don't deserve to be the Avatar.

"Accept that these things have happened, but do not let them poison your energy. If you are to be a positive influence on the world, you need to forgive yourself."

He's right. I can't change what I've done in the past, but I can try do better in the future—I hope.

"Remember how alive you felt at the moments of your greatest pleasure."

Immediately Katara's beautiful face filled

my vision and I was back in the Cave of Two Lovers. . . .

"Well, I sense that chakra just opened up like a dam!" Guru Pathik said.

Me too. I do forgive myself and I am ready to move on. I also can't wait to see Katara again!

Next came the Fire Chakra. It deals with willpower and is blocked by shame.

"What are you ashamed of? What are your biggest disappointments in yourself?" the guru asked.

I instantly saw myself struggling to learn Earthbending. Then my mind filled with my clumsy attempt at Firebending and how I burned Katara. It's clear to me now—I can't ever Firebend again. I can't risk hurting Katara or anyone else.

But when I told this to Guru Pathik, he told me I was wrong.

"You cannot deny this part of your life, Aang. You are the Avatar, and therefore you ARE a Firebender."

Right. I have to learn Firebending. There's no way around it.

I took a deep breath and pictured myself

easily controlling fire—no shame, no disappointment, just the strong will to get it right. Then I let out a burp.

"That chakra opened like a burping bison!" he remarked.

The fourth chakra was the Air Chakra. It deals with love and is blocked by grief.

Should be a piece of cake for a natural Airbender like me!

"Lay all your grief out in front of you."

Happy memories of when I was a little kid at the temple flooded my mind: when I first met Appa, when I started learning from Gyatso. Then, suddenly, Gyatso's laughing face melted into a bony skeleton. The grief bubbled up from deep inside, and tears streamed down my face.

Don't block the grief. Let it flow out.

Suddenly I was floating on a cloud in the sky surrounded by all the Air Nomads I knew growing up. They were all meditating, but as I passed each one, they disappeared. Gone, just like in real life. It was like losing them all over again. . . .

"You have indeed felt a great loss. But the love the Air Nomads had for you has not left this world. It is still inside your heart, and it is reborn in the form of new love."

There's Katara! There she is finding me frozen in the iceberg. Now it makes sense. Love never dies; it lives on inside me and makes it possible for me to love again.

The fifth chakra was the Sound Chakra. It deals with truth and is blocked by lies, the big lies we tell ourselves.

There's Katara and Sokka asking me why I didn't tell them right away that I was the Avatar. It was because I never wanted this responsibility.

"Then why do you accept it?"

It's my duty to bring balance to the world.

"Do you WANT this, or are you trying to impress someone else who thinks you SHOULD do this?"

Why is he asking me that? He's basically accusing me of not really wanting to be the Avatar. But I do want to be the Avatar! I think.

The visions of Katara and Sokka melted from my mind, and I was suddenly alone on a high mountaintop. I looked out at the world.

I do like being the Avatar. I WANT this. I know that now. The world is depending on me, and that's okay.

"Very good, Aang. You have opened your Sound Chakra to truth."

The sixth chakra was the Light Chakra. It deals with insight and is blocked by illusion. Guru Pathik explained that the big illusion is the illusion of separation. People are connected. So are the four nations. We are all one people. In fact, even the separation of the four elements is an illusion.

I opened my mind and saw an image of the four elements blending. Then the vision shifted to Toph Earthbending metal. I get it! The four elements are just four parts of the same whole. Even metal is just earth that has been changed into a different form. Just then the Light Chakra opened for me. One more to go.

"Once you open the final chakra, you'll be able to move in and out of the Avatar state at will. And you will have complete control and awareness of all your actions while in the Avatar state."

I am so psyched! This is why I came here. This is the big step that will allow me to defeat the Fire Lord and unite the world. Let's go. I'm ready!

The guru told me that the Thought Chakra deals with pure cosmic energy and is blocked by all earthly attachments.

"To begin, Aang, you must meditate on what attaches you to this world."

Instantly my mind filled with thoughts of Katara. I saw us together in all the things we've been through, and I realized that I'm never happier than when I'm with her.

"Now, let all of these attachments go," he continued. "Let them flow away, forgotten. . . . Learn to let her go, or you cannot let pure cosmic energy flow in from the universe."

What? What's he talking about? Why would I ever want to let go of Katara? I love her. This must be some kind of mistake. How can feeling an attachment to Katara be a bad thing? She means everything to me. I don't understand—and just when I thought this was going to be easy.

"I'm sorry, but I can't let go of Katara."

"Aang, you must clear all the chakras to master the Avatar state. The Thought Chakra is your gate to all the energy in the universe. You must trust it and surrender yourself."

I closed my eyes again, trying to let go. I saw myself walking on a narrow bridge over the universe. Katara was there with me on the bridge, but as I relaxed, she lifted into the sky, growing smaller and smaller until she became just one more glowing star in the cosmos. I turned around and saw this giant standing at the end of the bridge.

Wait. That giant is me, in the Avatar state. I get it now! I have to reach myself in the Avatar state to clear the Thought Chakra.

I walked toward the giant, but then, suddenly, I heard Katara screaming. I spun around and saw her bound in chains, locked in a prison.

Katara's in trouble. I'm certain of it. I have to save her.

But the giant Avatar also beckoned me.

What am I supposed to do? Do I continue to cleanse the final chakra and let go of Katara? Can I give up the person I love most in the world, or do I turn my back on learning to con—trol the Avatar state? I can't just ignore her! What if she's in real danger?

I turned away from the giant Avatar and ran across the bridge to where Katara was trapped, but the bridge crumbled beneath my feet and I fell into the vast emptiness of space, lost forever.

Then I opened my eyes. I was back with Guru Pathik. I jumped to my feet in a panic.

"Katara is in danger. I have to go!"

Guru Pathik told me that by choosing Katara, I had locked the last chakra.

"Aang, if you leave now, you won't be able to go into the Avatar state at all!"

Somewhere in a distant corner of my mind, a voice is telling me to stay and complete my journey. Sorry, voice, Katara's in trouble. I could never live with myself if anything happened to her that I could have prevented. I don't want to lose the power of the Avatar state, but if being the Avatar means that I have to give up everyone I love, maybe I don't want to be the Avatar after all. Isn't the Avatar SUPPOSED to do things like help people in danger? Maybe THIS is what I'm meant to do BECAUSE I'm the Avatar. Either way, I know I need to save Katara because I'm Aang. I have no choice.

I leaped onto Appa's back and took off for Ba Sing Se as fast as I could.

Chapter 13

On the way back to the city, I stopped and picked up Sokka. Then we spotted Toph below, surfing a wave of earth. Appa swooped down and we picked her up too. Sokka told us about how great it was to see his dad, and Toph told us that she learned how to bend metal! First I just thought, Gosh, she's such an amazing Earthbender. But then I thought about my visions with the guru, and how I'd seen Toph bending metal in one of them when I was trying to cleanse the Light Chakra. The Light Chakra is blocked by illusions, and just like the Waterbender from the swamp and the guru told me, time really must be an illusion, because the vision I saw in the swamp of Toph laughing and the vision I saw just a while ago of her bending metal both came true!

And all of this means that my vision of Katara must be real—she must really be in danger! It also probably means that the guru is right—my seventh chakra is blocked. Well, first things first, I guess. Both Toph and Sokka were upset when I told them about the vision of Katara, and we sped off for Ba Sing Se as quickly as Appa could take us there.

They asked me how my experience with the guru went. I lied to them and told them I completely mastered the Avatar state. As much as they love Katara, they won't understand my choice. They'll think I abandoned my responsibility. And maybe I did. I don't know. But what I do know is that I have to make sure Katara is okay. I also know that I had to lie about this. I don't feel good about it, but I can't deal with all this now. First Katara, then I'll figure out how to make all the Avatar stuff right—I hope.

We landed in Ba Sing Se and hurried to the king's throne room. But to my surprise he told me that Katara was off with the Kyoshi warriors and doing fine. We headed for our apartment, where I was greeted by Momo— but no Katara.

She IS in trouble. I knew it. My vision was right.

Then a knock came at the door. Toph threw open the door and there stood Zuko's uncle, Iroh!

This is the last thing I need, to battle Iroh. Is Zuko with him? Maybe they have Katara. . . .

It turned out that Toph and Iroh had met before, in the woods when Toph ran away from us, and they'd become friends.

"Toph, I need your help," Iroh said. "Princess Azula is in Ba Sing Se."

Azula! SHE must have Katara. Now I'm really worried. Azula nearly killed me the last time we fought. She's crazy, and super dangerous. How are we going to save Katara?

Iroh explained that Azula had captured Katara and Zuko.

"We'll work together to fight Azula and save Zuko and Katara," I said.

Sokka was shocked when I said we'd rescue Zuko. I guess I was a bit surprised myself. But I'm willing to do anything to save Katara, and after dealing with Azula, Zuko really didn't seem so bad.

Iroh brought along a Dai Li agent he had captured. The agent told us that Azula and Long Feng were plotting to overthrow the Earth King! He also said that Katara was being held in the crystal catacombs of old Ba Sing Se, deep beneath the palace.

Toph Earthbended a tunnel beneath the palace, then we split up. While Sokka and Toph went to warn the Earth King about Azula's coup, Iroh and I headed into the tunnel to rescue Katara and Zuko.

First I started actually feeling sorry for Zuko, now I'm trusting his uncle, a retired Fire Nation general. Boy, it's strange how things change. You think you have stuff all figured out, who's good and who's evil, and then people go and surprise you.

Toph's tunnel led us into a crystal courtyard, a wide-open plaza with waterfalls and a stream running over beautiful crystal rocks. I used Earthbending to open sections of the courtyard's walls until I finally found Katara's and Zuko's prison.

"Aang! I knew you would come!" Katara rushed over and hugged me.

Thank goodness she's okay! Now I know I made the right choice.

Just then Zuko rushed at me, but Iroh stopped him. Those two had a lot to talk about, so Katara and I left them and headed off to find Sokka and Toph.

But before we got out of the crystal court—yard, Azula attacked! She fired bolts of blue lightning. Katara countered by Waterbending water from the stream as I used Earthbending to block Azula's blasts and knock her off balance.

94

Azula may be too much for me alone, but working with Katara, I think I'm going to beat her. Wait, Zuko's back! Did his uncle convince him to help us or will he join Azula against us? I wonder what he'll choo—

BAM!

Zuko just sent a fire blast headed right at me! So much for people surprising me. Same old Zuko. Only now he's teamed with his ruthless sister! I hope we have what it takes to beat them. . . .

Oh, no! Katara's hurt. She just fell down into the stream. . . . Azula must have zapped her as she stepped into the water, shocking her! I didn't save her! I rejected Guru Pathik to save her and I still failed.

Now a troop of Dai Li agents are joining in the fight, throwing Earthbending attacks at me. There are too many of them. I can't stop them all AND beat Azula and Zuko.

Guru Pathik is right. I'm holding on to my earthly attachment and ruining everything. There's only one way to make this better: I have to let her go.

I'm sorry, Katara.

I Earthbended a protective crystal shell around myself, and then I began to meditate.

I'm back on that bridge, walking toward the giant version of myself in the Avatar state. . . .

Don't hesitate this time; just walk toward the giant Aang. Accept your fate. . . .

It's working! I'm slipping into the Avatar state! I feel more powerful than I ever have before!

BOOM!

What's that? What hit me? Oh, no. The bridge, it's crumbling beneath my feet. . . . I'm falling. . . .

I could hear Katara's voice drifting softly through the darkness. Then I felt myself slowly waking up. In my mind I saw a glowing band of golden water soothing me, restoring me.

When I finally opened my eyes, I was stretched out on Appa's back, flying away from Ba Sing Se. Katara kneeled over me, healing me with her Waterbending. I hugged her and we both started to cry. She told me that Iroh had helped us escape. I guess some people will still surprise me after all.

When I sat up, I saw that Sokka, Toph, and the Earth King were with us. The Earth King looked down at the city and sighed.

"The Earth Kingdom has fallen," he said solemnly.

Everything was my fault—again. What if I had made a different choice? What if I had been able to give up Katara the first time, cleansed my chakra, and gained control of the Avatar state? Maybe the Earth Kingdom would now be free. Maybe Azula and Zuko would be defeated. Maybe the war would be over.

But it isn't. I have to find a way to make all this right. I just hope I can find the strength to figure out how. . . .